At the Wheel

I Want to Drive a

Snowplow

Henry Abbot

illustrated by
Aurora Aguilera

PowerKiDS press.

New York

Published in 2017 by The Rosen Publishing Group, Inc.
29 East 21st Street, New York, NY 10010

First Edition

Managing Editor: Nathalie Beullens-Maoui
Editor: Theresa Morlock
Book Design: Michael Flynn
Illustrator: Aurora Aguilera

Cataloging-in-Publication Data

Names: Abbot, Henry, author.
Title: I want to drive a snowplow / Henry Abbot.
Description: New York : PowerKids Press, [2017] | Series: At the wheel |
  Includes index.
Identifiers: LCCN 2016027641| ISBN 9781499426663 (pbk. book) | ISBN
  9781508152651 (6 pack) | ISBN 9781499429428 (library bound book)
Subjects: LCSH: Snowplows–Juvenile literature.
Classification: LCC TD868 .A23 2017 | DDC 625.7/63–dc23
LC record available at https://lccn.loc.gov/2016027641

Manufactured in the United States of America

CPSIA Compliance Information: Batch #BW17PK: For Further Information contact Rosen Publishing, New York, New York at 1-800-237-9932

Contents

Lots of Snow 4

Big Truck 10

Pushing and Scooping 18

Words to Know 24

Index 24

I want to drive a snowplow.
What would it be like?

5

It snowed a lot overnight. When I wake up, the town is covered in snow.

8

It's time for the snowplow
to get to work! I'm going to
drive it today.

9

A snowplow is a
big truck.

It has a plow
in front.

11

I have to climb stairs to get
in the snowplow.

That's how big it is!

I turn on the snowplow.

Then I pull it out on to the street.

15

The snowplow has big,
thick wheels. They easily
roll over snow and ice.

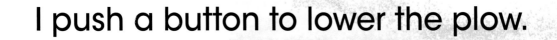

I push a button to lower the plow.

18

It pushes snow out of the way.

I push another button. The plow scoops
the snow off the ground. Wow!

My snowplow makes the streets clear and safe. It's fun to drive a snowplow!

23

Words to Know

plow

snow

wheels

Index

B
button, 18, 21

P
plow, 11, 18, 21

S
snow, 7, 16, 19, 21

W
wheels, 16